RICHIE AND I HUDDLED together and pressed
our faces into the cold glass of the Hudson's store window.
Everywhere we looked was a dazzling array of wondrous toys
for Christmas. Then my eyes fell on the most beautiful thing
I'd ever seen: a delicate ballerina doll, her hair drawn up in a
nest of perfect curls held there by a halo of tiny blue flowers.
Her slippers were gold, like polished stars. How I longed to
have her!

My brother was eyeing the sleek black model steam train
poised on gleaming silver tracks. "Looks like the 922," he
sighed as he flattened his nose against the glass.

Our warm breath made misty clouds on the window.

# Gifts

## of the

# PATRICIA POLACCO

# Heart

G. P. Putnam's Sons • An Imprint of Penguin Group (USA) Inc.

Well, you two," Grampa's voice called out as our Model A rumbled home. "We need to get home before the lady from the Agency gets there." Grampa was trying to be cheerful, but we knew his heart was heavy. This was going to be our last Christmas on the farm.

Gramma had died in the fall and he was selling the farm in the spring. Too many memories! Stone for stone and board for board, Grampa'd built the place with his two hands. He always told us that before he and Gramma

moved into the house, they'd breathed magic into it—and the very ground it stood on. We believed him.

"Is that the lady from the Agency?" Richie asked as we pulled up to the house. There was someone standing by the back door.

"That's her! What with your momma taking that teaching job in Battle Creek and getting home so late, we need someone to take care of you two!" Grampa said.

"I don't want any ol' lady we don't know in Gramma's house," Richie whispered.

Richie was right! A very strange-looking woman was standing by the back door. It was snowing and the flakes swirled around her like a soft white cloak.

As we walked up to her, she smiled. "The name's Kay Lamity. I'm yer new housekeeper!" she said, and she spun on her heels and trundled through the side door into the kitchen.

"Fine kitchen!" she crowed with approval. "Which one of you young'uns is going to show me where your gramma kept everything? I got to get to cookin'!"

Richie dropped into a chair at the table. "You talk funny . . . where you from?"

"Yazoo, Mississippi," she exclaimed as she rolled up her sleeves.

"You know what your name means, don't you?" he added through squinted eyes.

"Sure do. Means I'll be shakin' things up 'round here, I 'spect." She grinned.

"*Ca-lamity* means 'disaster'!" Richie said defiantly. "Disaster."

Grampa hurried up. "Oh, I apologize for the rudeness of my grandson," he said, giving Richie a you'd-best-behave look.

"This is Gramma's kitchen," Richie mumbled.

Kay Lamity made us a fine dinner that night. All the cooking had fallen on Grampa after Gramma died, and now Momma didn't get home till late. We'd been living on scrambled eggs! Kay Lamity made fried chicken, gravy and mashed potatoes, with some corn that Gramma had canned last spring.

Dessert was best of all—scrumptious bread pudding! Momma's and my favorite.

"This here is clean outta your gramma's recipe box," Kay Lamity said.

But Richie pushed out from his chair, his face red and angry. "Maybe all of you are letting her take Gramma's place, but I ain't . . . I ain't never!" He thundered upstairs to his room and slammed the door.

Momma looked hurt and Grampa was angry. I started to cry.

"I'll remedy this," Kay Lamity said quietly and bounded up the stairs and burst into Richie's room. I followed behind her.

"Boy," she said, "where I come from, we cook yard-long night crawlers in green bugger gravy! And fer dessert, blister-pus puddin' with black widow garnish."

Richie looked up from his pillow.

"I can stare down an armadilla while dancin' on the back of a wild boar and tussle a gator to the ground while whistlin' 'Sweet Land o' Dixie,'" she said, crossing her arms and wagging her head.

Richie leaned forward and tried not to smile.

"And I play the meanest game of checkers this side of the sweet Mason-Dixon Line!"

"Bet you can't beat me," Richie whispered.

"Can too!" she countered.

"Can not!" he challenged with a slight smile.

"Well, slap my face to the side of a hog and let him roll in the mud. Let's go on downstairs and see if'n you can." That was the beginning of one sweet friendship.

It wasn't two days later that Grampa, Richie and I went out and cut down a tree for the parlor. Kay Lamity sank the bottom of it into a bucket of sand. We got out all of the ornaments, set a fire in the fireplace and sang songs while we decorated the tree.

"My favorite part of Christmas is this right here—bein' with family, a cracklin' fire and singin' down the moon." Kay Lamity sighed. "What's yours?" she asked me.

"When I hear Santa and his reindeer on the roof." I was thinking about that doll with the blue flowers in her hair.

Richie gave me a disgusted look and shook his head.

"Well, Richie boy, what exactly do you like about Christmas, then?"

"I like getting gifts, you know, presents!" he piped up. I knew he was thinking of that train.

Kay Lamity got a faraway look. "You know, they's gifts, and they's *gifts*."

Richie and I looked surprised. "Our gramma used to say that very thing."

"All them toys ya see in them shop windas are one kind of gift . . . Maybe they ain't the ones that count."

Richie and I looked at each other—could she read our minds?

"Gifts that come straight from the heart, that's the kind that's kept forever!"

"What do you mean . . . from the heart?" Richie asked her.

"A gift of the heart ain't opened by pullin' on a fancy bow or rippin' pretty paper off a box. It's about openin' your *heart* . . . and givin' what's inside. That's the greatest gift of all!"

The next morning, Grampa took Richie and me into town to shop.
As we motored over the bridge, we could see our good old village was
all a-bustle. Shopkeepers were putting the finishing touches on their
windows. People were hanging garlands of greens on the lampposts that
lined Main Street.

"Looks like they're getting ready for the Santa parade on Christmas
Eve," Grampa announced.

We shopped first, then stopped in the Sweet Shop. Grampa bought
us cinnamon gumdrops and popped them into our mouths, whispering,
"Sweets for the sweets."

When we pulled the door open to leave the shop, though, there in the doorway was Santa himself!

"Ho, ho, ho," he bellowed. "And have you two been good children?"

Richie shook his head yes. I was speechless. His suit was a little threadbare and had been patched. His beard was sparse, but none of that mattered to me. There Santa was, in all his glory!

"See!" I whispered to Richie.

Santa reached into a tattered brown bag and pulled out two Hershey bars and handed them to us. All the way home, I held that chocolate bar in my hand. I didn't want to eat it. It was from *him*.

When we got home, I couldn't wait to tell Kay Lamity all about seeing Santa, but Richie blustered, "That wasn't Santa—that was ol' man Barkoviac. He was wearing the same old broken watch that he always wears! There ain't no Santa, just old men who go around dressin' up like him."

I started crying so hard, I couldn't catch my breath. Grampa sent Richie to bed without supper.

Kay Lamity pulled me up on her lap. "Sweet little lamb," she began, "your brother is just upset. He didn't mean it."

"I know he did . . . and he isn't lying either," I sputtered. "I saw Mr. Barkoviac's watch, too. There really isn't a Santa."

Momma and Grampa looked at each other and their eyes were sad.

Later that night, after I had gone to bed, Kay Lamity sneaked a warm bowl of soup and toast to my brother. "That there soup is made from cockroach toes, bees' knees and buzzard bowels," she said as she put the tray in front of him.

Then she said, "Richie boy, we gotta have a talk." Richie just sipped his soup. "Tellin' that little girl that Santa ain't real has all but cast her adrift in an angry sea."

"Why does it matter to her so much what I say, anyway?" Richie quietly retorted.

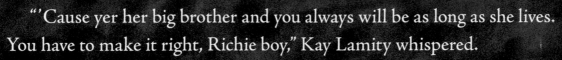

"'Cause yer her big brother and you always will be as long as she lives. You have to make it right, Richie boy," Kay Lamity whispered.

"How?" Richie asked as tears filled his eyes.

"What do you think yer little sister wants more than anything right now?" Kay Lamity asked him.

"For me to believe," he whispered softly. "But how can I do that if I don't?"

Kay Lamity opened the curtains so that Richie could see the bright stars. "Open your heart. That's all you gotta do," she whispered.

Then they looked at the night sky together.

The next night, both of us slept in Gramma's bed right next to the living room. It was warmer there by the fireplace.

"I want to show you something," Richie whispered as he pulled me out of bed and over to the window. The stars were especially bright, but one in particular seemed so much brighter. It twinkled and flashed.

"Kay Lamity showed me that star last night. I think it's Gramma's star," Richie said wistfully. Gramma had told us just before she died that stars were holes in the sky and that the light we see is the brightness of heaven showing through from the other side.

"Remember, she said that she was going there and that she would watch over us always," Richie added softly. Then he thought for a long time. "I know Santa's real, Trisha, 'cause Gramma told me herself. I just got mean 'cause I felt like no one was remembering her."

I almost thought Richie was going to cry.

"Look, Richie! The brightest star, it's flickering. It's Gramma. I know it is."

We hugged and climbed into bed and drifted off to sleep.

The next morning was Christmas Eve. The Santa parade was that night. I could hardly wait. But I was just finishing up breakfast, when I called out, "Richie! What are we going to get Momma and Grampa for Christmas?"

"Well, we ain't got no money, so we can't buy them anything . . ." Richie started to say when Kay Lamity spun around from the sink.

"Don't you two remember what I said about heart gifts? You'll be needin' to find some this Christmas. Maybe it's something from the farm . . . something that comes from the magic soil it stands on." She went right on peeling potatoes.

Richie and I pulled on our snowsuits and bolted out the door. We pulled

his sled through the pasture next to the barn. A tree was too big. Pinecones were nice but not special. Snow crystals wouldn't last. We just couldn't come up with a heart gift.

That's when I saw them. "Stop, Richie!" I said. "There!"

"Where?" Richie strained his eyes to see.

"There, peeking out of the snow . . . dried cornstalks." Pretty as anything.

Richie and I picked as many as we could hold.

"So we won't forget this farm for a long time," I whispered softly. "Kay Lamity will know just what to do with them."

We hurried back to the house to show Kay Lamity what we had chosen.

"Perfect!" she crowed. "Now I'll show you something magic we can make from these . . . true gifts of the heart!"

We all toiled for what seemed like hours. But our fingers and hearts soared. We cut, pasted, drew and sewed. Kay Lamity sewed small pouches that we filled with soil from our farm and attached to our gifts.

Then we wrapped them and placed them under the tree in the parlor.

Later that night, Grampa bundled all of us into the car, heading for town
to see the Christmas parade. I could hardly wait to see Santa.

As we approached town, we could see everyone was there lining the
streets. Richie pulled me through the crowd to take another look at the toy
store window. I caught my breath again when I saw the ballerina doll with
those beautiful curls piled on her head. Richie didn't take his eyes off that
black steam engine on its gleaming tracks.

Then we heard the crowd cheering. When we turned around, we couldn't

see Momma, Grampa or Kay Lamity anywhere. Just the floats going by. Then one of the millions of kids called out, "There's Santa!"

The crowd rushed to the edge of the street to see him. But I lost my balance and fell! Richie tried to help me up, but some bigger kids crowded in front of me. "I can't see! I can't see!" I shouted. Neither of us could hardly get a glimpse of him. All I managed to see was Santa's arm waving above the crowd.

Grampa pulled me up and put me on his shoulders. But it was too late— Santa was already across the bridge and turning down another road.

I wept silently as we chugged down Dunks Road on our way home to our farm. "I didn't see him," I said, sniffling.

Kay Lamity turned and looked at me. "Baby dear, can you see the wind as it blows? Can you see how a flower smells in the springtime? Can you see how much your momma and grampa love you?"

"I guess not," I sputtered.

"Well, then, just because you didn't see Santa don't mean that he ain't there just the same."

I knew she was right, righter than rain. I instantly felt better. That was when Richie started noticing a star again. This one was twinkling just over Ollie Arbogast's meadow. Its light got brighter and brighter. Brighter even than Gramma's star.

"Grampa, look!" Richie called out.

"What? . . . What!" Grampa almost swerved off the road.

"The light. There, right above us!" I squealed.

Grampa stopped his car and got out. All of us were transfixed, looking up at something that none of us could explain, and we watched it until we couldn't see it anymore.

"Did you hear sleigh bells?" Kay Lamity asked. "Maybe it's headin' for the farm!"

"Trisha, we have to get home to bed," Richie crowed. We just knew it had to be Santa and he wouldn't be coming unless we were there.

We thundered through the door, climbed into our pajamas and jumped into Gramma's bed.

"Now listen fer them bells," Kay Lamity whispered. She closed the door.

We lay there for the longest time trembling with pure excitement. We may have fallen asleep, when we were jarred awake by the sound of something far off. Was it bells? Again? It was! Bells coming from the north.

Then we both heard a bump on the roof. We did! Then we heard new sounds, like someone walking around.

"I know it was Santa we saw up in the sky," I whispered.

"And now he's here!" Richie whispered back.

We lay there without saying a word until all we could hear was our own breathing.

Christmas morning, Richie and I tumbled into the parlor and crawled under the tree. There, bathed in her own light, was the glorious ballerina doll. When I looked at my brother, he was holding a small train. Not a model, a train exactly like the 922. We heard Grampa, Momma and Kay Lamity whispering about where these expensive toys could possibly have come from. Richie and I knew!

Then Richie and I dove under the tree to get the gifts that we made for everyone.

"They are corn husk angels made from the cornstalks we grew right here on our farm, Grampa!" I chirped. Grampa got tears in his eyes.

"Kay Lamity helped us sew these little pouches around their necks . . . we filled them with the magic soil from our fields," Richie added. Momma was speechless.

"We made one especially for you, Kay Lamity," Richie whispered.

She held it next to her heart.

"These will help us remember our farm forever," I said quietly.

Richie and I pulled on our snowsuits to build a snowman before Christmas breakfast. He bolted out the front door and was running ahead of me.

"Oh, Richie, do you think Santa was really here?"

As he turned to answer me, he looked shocked. "Trisha, look!" He pointed at the roof of our house. There on that steep little roof were two runner marks in the snow as if made by a sleigh! And it sure looked like

hoof marks between them—some of them leading right to the chimney!

We stood there for the longest time, almost unable to move or breathe, when Richie pointed at the yard. There were more of those runner marks with lots and lots of hoof marks between them!

"Here's where his sleigh was pulled along." Richie was following the marks in the snow. "Then . . . look. They just stop."

"As if they lifted off the ground and flew away."

That's when I saw something in the snow that was dark, leathery and partially buried. I picked it up. It was a piece of broken harness with two bells attached to it. "Santa's bells," I whispered breathlessly.

Then both of us just stood and looked at the sky in wonder.

And Kay Lamity? When the farm sold in the spring, she moved—back to Yazoo, Mississippi, she told us. But one day Grampa met the lady from the Agency. We'd been wanting to thank her for bringing us Kay.

"Kay Lamity?" she said. "I'm afraid I've never heard of her!"

She said when we never came to the Agency, she figured we had decided we didn't need any extra help after all.

I figured it didn't matter. When we drove back to the farm that day, I decided Kay Lamity was the real gift, a true gift of the heart. And as long as I live, I'll believe that.

*For my family and the mysterious wonder they created in all of our lives.*

*Patricia Lee Gauch, Editor*

G. P. Putnam's Sons
An imprint of Penguin Young Readers Group
Published by The Penguin Group
Penguin Group (USA) Inc., 375 Hudson Street, New York, NY 10014, USA

USA | Canada | UK | Ireland | Australia | New Zealand | India | South Africa | China
Penguin Books Ltd, Registered Offices: 80 Strand, London WC2R 0RL, England
For more information about the Penguin Group, visit penguin.com

Library of Congress Cataloging-in-Publication Data
Polacco, Patricia, author, illustrator.
Gifts of the heart / Patricia Polacco.  pages cm   Summary: Kay Lamity, Trisha and Richie's new housekeeper, shows them
how special it is to give Christmas gifts that come from the heart.  [1. Christmas—Fiction. 2. Gifts—Fiction.] I. Title.
PZ7.P75186Gi 2013  [E]—dc23  2012048016

Published simultaneously in Canada. Manufactured in China by South China Printing Co. Ltd.
ISBN 978-0-399-16094-3
1 3 5 7 9 10 8 6 4 2

Design by Semadar Megged.  Text set in 15/20 point Adobe Jenson Pro.
The illustrations are rendered in pencils and markers.
The publisher does not have any control over and does not assume any responsibility for author
or third-party websites or their content.